I0530872

Joy

Is This the End?

By Kimberly Kirby

Kimberly Kirby

www.KimJKirby.com

Kimberly Kirby

DEDICATION

Dedicated to all who have supported my dream by listening, reading, critiquing my work, or purchasing my stories. You have my eternal love and gratitude.

From my heart to yours,

Kimberly Kirby

Joy: Is this the End?

.

Kimberly Kirby

CHAPTER 1

Joy slowly sits on the examination table. As she lies back, the bright fluorescent lights shine down on her face causing her to look away. The white paper covering the table rustles in her ear as she scoots around to get comfortable.

"So how is our little mommy?" Dr. Karen asks smiling down at Joy. She knows how much Joy hates all the "cutesy" talk.

Joy rolls her eyes and smiles back at her.

"I'm fine, Dr. Karen, thank you. Just having some pain in my back lately."

"And she's eating anything she can get her hands on!" Jonathan chimes in. He lets out a hearty laugh.

Joy gives him a vicious sideways stare and he quickly shuts up.

"Oh lighten up, girl! Enjoy your pregnancy! This is the only time in your life when people will tell you to eat more than you should and they won't care if you get fat." She pats Joy on the shoulder.

"Ok, let's get started." Dr. Karen says as she squeezes a cold gel on Joys tummy.

She runs the wand of the ultrasound machine across the gel. The room is suddenly filled with the thumping of the baby's heartbeat. An image of the tiny fetus can now be seen on the monitor.

Jonathan reaches out and squeezes Joy's hand. A wave of emotion washes over him bringing tears to his eyes. He fights them back and smiles down at Joy.

"Man, I can't believe I'm going to be a father," Jon says with a chuckle.

"Yea, it is pretty cool, huh?" Joy smiles back at him.

"Definitely, I'm so glad you're letting me be involved this time, because . . ." Jon starts but is interrupted as Dr. Karen chimes in.

"This time?" She blurts out, confused.

"Umm, Karen, I need to talk to you about some personal things for a moment," Joy jumps in trying not to let the panic show on her face.

"Jon, can you give us a minute?" Joy turns to him and gestures for him to leave the room.

"Uh, yea. You ok?" He asks before exiting.

"I'm fine, just some . . um . . feminine stuff I wanna talk about in private." She scrambles to come up with anything to get him out of the room.

"Oh, I'll give you some privacy," he mumbles awkwardly as he makes his way out of the room and closes the door behind him.

"What did he mean by, this time?" Dr Karen asks again.

"Nothing, could you just finish the exam, please? We are not here to discuss my personal life!" Joy snaps as she lies back on the examination table.

"Sure," Dr. Karen eyes Joy suspiciously.

"We want to make sure the baby is healthy, this time." Dr. Karen replies, smugly.

Carla relaxes on her plush beige couch in the living room of her home. She sits back and lets her head rest on the back of the sofa as she sips her white wine and stares blankly at the flames dancing in the fireplace.

At that moment she hears Albert coming in through the front door. She straightens up and crosses her legs toward the door.

"And how are you, darling?" She smirks arrogantly as he crosses through the room to get to the stairs leading up to his bedroom.

Albert stomps through the room silently, his jaw tightens as he heads up the stairs without a word to his wife.

The past few months have been extremely tense in the Waters' household. Carla and Albert are in the middle of a very nasty divorce. Albert is detesting the conditions under which he signed over half of his fortune and his house to Carla.

Unfortunately, since he has no proof that his wife purposely triggered an allergic reaction that almost killed him and forced him to sign the papers, he's been having a rough time in court.

Since the trial is still ongoing, he has not been forced to vacate his home. At least until the terms of the divorce are settled.

Albert has, however, moved out of their bedroom. He now permanently sleeps in the guestroom down the hall. That is, when he's not sleeping over at Heathers'.

As Carla watches her husband stomp up the stairs and out of view, her smile suddenly begins to crack. She relaxes back onto the couch and refocuses her gaze on the dancing flames. A single tear rolls down her cheek. She quickly wipes it away, picks up her glass and finishes her wine.

Angela sits quietly in the third pew as she stares lovingly at Will. She can't help but to blush as she watches him deliver the word during the Wednesday night bible study. Her heart flutters every time he glances in her direction.

"Please turn your bibles to Genesis chapter two." Will's booming voice announces from the pulpit.

Angela grabs her bible and quickly flips to Genesis, she notices a small piece of paper fall from her bible and gently land in her lap. Figuring it for trash she begins to ball it up and shove it in her purse until she notices the writing on it.

As she unfolds it, she reads:
"You make every breath worth it. I love you. - Will"

As Angela stares at the small piece of paper a smile begins to spread across her face.

"And God said, It's not good that man should be alone....." Will continues.

Angela is startled out of her daydream when she realizes Will is standing over her.

"Church, I've been alone for a long time . . . and that's hard for a minister. You know, we're expected to pour out everything that God has given us on a daily basis. We're visiting the sick, studying the word to make sure we can bring forth a powerful message every week. I mean, we're counseling people and comforting people all the time when sometimes we need that comfort. We need that listening ear. "

Will's jaw clenches as he tries to fight back the emotion.

"Do you know how it feels to be strong and offer your shoulder for everybody else to cry, and feel like you have no one to cry to? It's hard, church! And it's lonely. That is why God says it's not good for us to be alone."

Angela notices the tears in Will's eyes. Her heart aches for him. She had no idea that the ministry weighed on him so heavily.

"Church let me encourage you today. Continue to trust Him, continue to believe that no matter what you're going through God hears you and He cares about you."

Will takes a deep breath and smiles to himself.

"He sent me someone, someone that I can talk to. Someone who gives me that shoulder when I need it. Y'all, he sent a woman into my life at a time when I was ready to give up on finding someone for myself."

Will reaches into his jacket pocket and pulls out a small black box. He grabs Angela's hand and slowly helps her to her feet.

At this point Angela can't even hear the words that are pouring out of her man's mouth. The huge sanctuary of Life Overcomers Church suddenly feels the size of a closet. She feels her palms drenched in sweat. She frantically tries to wipe them on her dress but nothing seems to help. She can feel each pair of eyes in the room watching her as her heart beats out of her chest.

She stands there frozen, trying to forget everyone else in the room and focus on Will.

Will kneels before Angela and slowly stares at her as he wipes the tears from his eyes.

"Angela Harris, I believe that you are the woman God has purposed to stand beside me. I feel like I've loved you from the first moment I saw you. Will you marry me?"

Angela snaps out of her trance in time to hear the words that she's wanted to hear for the last twenty years of her life.

However, she had always imagined it would be David uttering those words to her.

Angela stares down at the man who gives her heart exactly what it needs and she says exactly what she knows his heart needs to hear, "Yes".

Joy wanders around Walmart searching for the baby clothes and finally stumbles upon them in the rear of the store. She forced Jonathan to bring her here to stock up on all of her favorite junk food before he dropped her off at home after their movie date.

Since she found out she was pregnant, she hasn't been able to bring herself to buy anything for the baby. That would make it too real. Which means that in just a few months, Joy, would be a mother. She wasn't ready to face it all yet.

She notices the cutest package of onesies.

"Ducks," she whispers and smiles as she runs her fingers over the embroidered ducklings.

She grabs the package from the shelf, notices the most adorable blue jump suit, for a child of at least a year, and snatches it from the rack. She combs through the racks grabbing anything that isn't nailed down; baby booties, rattles, brushes, diaper bags , and etc.

"Joy!" Jonathan calls her name snapping her out of her frenzy.

"I think I got everything on your list, but I couldn't find the double stuffed Oreos." He says, as he makes his way over to her with a basket full of snacks.

Joy stands there frozen, her arms filled with every baby item she could carry. She stares at Jon unable to speak.

"Babe, you ok?" He notices the panic on her face.

She opens her mouth to speak but the words won't come quick enough.

"I . . . I'm not ready to be . . . a mother." She finally blurts out.

Jon rushes to her side and slowly begins taking each item from her and placing them on the diaper rack next to them.

"Of course not babe. I'm not ready to be a father. We didn't plan this, it just happened." Jon says as he grabs her hand.

"I know we didn't plan it! But it's happening, how am I supposed to raise a child? I'm nineteen years old!" Joy yells at him, her eyes begging for an answer.

Jonathan pulls her close to him and wraps his arms around her.

"Look , I've been kinda feeling the same way. I don't know how we're gonna do this, but I know it's gonna work out. I read somewhere that it's all about instincts, you know. Its kinda like everything we need to know, we already know. And whatever we don't . . . we can ask our moms." Jonathan says with a reassuring smile.

Joy smiles back at him as she stares into his comforting eyes. He always had a way of making everything better. He just had that way about him.

"You're right" she says grabbing his hand. Let's get out of here, these people probably think I'm nuts."

Carla finds herself sitting in her car outside of Albert's office, again. Every now and then she can grab a glimpse of him as he passes through the hallway.

She wipes away a lone tear as it glides down her face. She never wanted things to go this far. All she wanted was to get her marriage back on track, but when she heard Albert whispering about leaving her for good, that night on the balcony, she was filled with rage.

Her anger has always gotten her into trouble but she's always been able to charm her way out of any lasting damage. This time, however, she might have gone too far.

As Carla rests her head on the seat, her eyes still locked on the building, she's startled out of her trance by a red Mercedes as it zips into the parking lot. She watches as the driver pulls into a parking space on the side of the building.

Carla notices Heather peak out of the window at the Mercedes, seconds later she scampers out of the building, rushes over to the car and gets in.

"Damn it," Carla says noticing the windows are too dark to see who is inside.

Carla watches the car for about five minutes. Just as she has resolved that she'll never know who's inside, the window slowly begins to roll down.

A man hangs his arm outside of the vehicle as he takes a drag from a cigarette.

"That little bitch is cheating on him!" Carla happily exclaims as she stares intently at the Mercedes.

"I knew it, Gold digging tramp!" She mumbles to herself as she fishes around in her purse for her cell phone to take a picture.

As she tries to focus the camera her smile fades as she realizes all she can see is the pale white arm of the driver and his short blonde hair. She can't even see his face nor can she see Heather.

She tosses the phone into the passenger seat as she grunts in frustration.

Heather hops out of the car and the driver quickly speeds away.

"Hmph!" Carla sighs. She can still see Heather hustling around the office.

Carla slides on her Prada shades as she speeds out of the parking lot.

The roar of canned laughter snaps Angela out of her sleep. She feels around her plush, ruby red comforter for the remote. With one eye open she clicks the power button and flings the remote to the other side of the bed. She pulls the covers over her head and begins to dose off.

Before she can drift off her cell phone begins to ring.

"Ugh!" She grunts as she snatches the phone without looking at it.

"Hello?" she mumbles as she lays her head back on the pillow and closes her eyes.

"What's up?" David responds.

Angela's eyes fling open as she sits up in her bed. She hasn't spoken to David in three months. She's been dodging his phone calls and text messages in an attempt to get him out of her system.

"Ah man, she's still alive," David chuckles to himself. "I was beginning to get worried about you."

"Well, um, I'm fine. Just busy." She says, fumbling to pull her words together.

"Busy, huh? I remember when you always had time for me." He replies cockily.

"Well, a lots changed, David. You can't just call my house all hours of the night. What do you want?" Angela says as she twists her engagement ring around on her finger.

"Oh so you making changes now? Am I one of the changes?" He asks, in a sincere tone.

"Yes, I can say without a doubt that you are one of those changes." Angela blurts out sternly.

"Damn, a nigga can't get a phone call . . . nah, damn a phone call. You could've told me face to face. That's the least you could've done, hell I think you owe me that much." He lashes out angrily.

"No, David! The least I could've done is exactly what the hell I did, nothing! I don't owe you anything. " Angela yells, matching his arrogant tone.

"Ah, hell naw!" David laughs.

"He must be knocking the bottom outta that thang!" He jabs.

"That's none of your damn business!" She yells, feeling the tears in her eyes.

"Since when is it none of my business? It was my business when you had me up in that thang doing his job." He boasts.

"Since now! Since he proposed to me!" Angela screams, her hand trembling as she clenches the phone.

David's haughty laughter quickly screeches to a halt.

"What you mean proposed? Y'all getting married?"

"Yes, married. What, you surprised someone wants to marry me?" Speaking of which, where is your fiancé?" She says, with more confidence than before.

"Man, I wasn't gon' marry that girl. I guess she figured it out quicker than I thought she would." David answers.

He quickly brings the conversation back to Angela.
"How you gon' marry somebody you ain't never slept wit? Unless y'all *are* sleeping together." He digs.

"Like I said, that part of my life is no longer your business. As a matter of fact, you shouldn't even be calling me unless it's about Jonathan. Or, better yet, why don't you try calling your son. When is the last time you talked to him? Goodbye David."

Angela quickly hangs up the phone before he can respond. She can't risk letting him suck her in again. She stares down at her ring and then glances over to a picture of her and Will on her nightstand. She smiles to herself as she tosses her phone on the nightstand.

Joy, Jonathan, and Chris meet up for lunch at Applebee's. The waitress shows them to a four top table where Jon flops down on one side. Joy happily takes the seat across from him and grabs his hand. Chris heads toward the chair near Jon, he pauses for a brief moment with his eyes locked on Joy. He quickly doubles back and grabs the seat next to her.

Joy gives him a vicious side eye before turning her attention back to Jonathan.

Joy has been doing her best to ignore Chris despite her overwhelming attraction to him. Something about the way he licks his lips and gives her that sideways smile drives her insane.

Joy snatches her water from the waitress before she can set it on the table and begins to chug it down.

"Damn girl, You alright?" Jon says, as he and Chris share a boisterous laugh at her expense.

"I'm fine." Joy scoffs, as she grabs her menu to avoid them both.

"You sure you ok, you been actin' tense all day." Chris says as he places his hand on her knee and slowly inches up her thigh.

"Yea, I'm fine." Joy mumbles, her eyes still glued to her menu.

She can't bring herself to move his hand.

For the past few months she's been doing everything in her power to avoid him. She never allows herself to be alone with him. Yet every time she closes her eyes to kiss Jon, she sees Chris' face.

"Babe, order me some ribs when the waitress comes back. Going to the bathroom." Jon hops up from the table and saunters off.

"Why have you been avoiding me?" Chris slides in closer to Joy and tightens his grip on her thigh.

Joys' heart begins pounding.

"I'm not avoiding you," she says, afraid to look at him. Her eyes stay dead locked on the menu though she's never wanted him more than she does right now.

"I can't take this, If I have to watch him kiss you or touch you one more time I'm gonna lose it on his ass! You are supposed to be with me! I know you want me, you can't even look at me!"

"I have no problem looking at . . ." she starts. As soon as their eyes lock Chris grabs and kisses her; running his hand past her baby bump to her breast.

Joy pushes him off and grabs her menu.

" Damn baby, you don't even want him." Chris snatches the menu and slams it on the table.

"You don't know what I want," Joy says, with tears in her eyes.

"Yes I do, I know you want me." Chris says, in a low tone as Jon approaches the table.

CHAPTER 2

Carla paces outside of the guestroom where Albert has been staying for the past few months. She nervously debates whether or not to knock on the door. She desperately wishes that they can have one conversation that doesn't end in screaming and throwing things.

She takes a deep breath, taps on the door, and slowly pushes it open.

Albert, is relaxing, in a dark brown recliner near the window, reading a book. He glances at her briefly and returns his gaze back to his book.

"What is it?" he grunts.

Carla moves inside of the room and props herself against the door frame.

"I made way too much food again, guess I'm still not used to cooking for one person. Joy is hardly ever home for dinner nowadays. You hungry?" Carla asks trying not let him hear the nervousness in her voice.

Albert looks at her over his reading glasses.

"You don't seriously think I'm going to eat your cooking again, do you?"

Carla gives him an uncomfortable laugh.

"Oh . . . right . . ." she smiles awkwardly.
She eases her way further into the room and slowly sits on the bed.

"That's not the only reason I came up here. I wanted to talk to you."

"Alright, go ahead." Albert never takes his eyes off of his book.

"What would you say if I told you I was willing to withdraw my petition to get half of your money?" Carla blurts out the words before she can talk herself out of it.

Albert, stunned, looks at her in disbelief. He searches for the right words but can only eek out, "Why?"

"Because I'm sorry, because I know how much I hurt you and have hurt you over the years. Look, I wasn't thinking! I overheard you talking about leaving me and going off to be with her . . . I was angry."

"Are you serious?" Albert asks, as he slides off his glasses and sits straight in his chair.

"Yes, but I do have some conditions. Look, I know I haven't been a great wife to you and I took you for granted. But, I was young and immature. I just wasn't ready to be anyone's wife. I'm ready now, Albert. And I still love you." Tears begin to roll down her face.

"It's not about the money, Albert. I just want you.

She inches closer to him.

"So, if you're willing to put some real effort into our marriage counseling and giving us another try, I'll drop everything."

Albert stares at his wife, over the past few months they have been in the most intense legal battle he ever imagined. There have been numerous times when he wanted to just walk away and let her have everything she asked for.

"You really expect me to believe that you think there's hope for our marriage?" Albert asks.

"Honestly, I don't know what I expect you to believe. All I know for sure is that I do want to try." Carla gives him a half smile and walks out of the room, closing the door behind her.

Angela stares at the bills piled up on her kitchen table. She jots down on a note pad how much she thinks she can pay towards each one.

She picks up her light bill which has the words, **"Cut Off Notice,"** written across the top in bold red letters.

At that moment, she hears a knock at the door. She hops up and opens the door. Will grabs her, kissing her before she can speak.

"Aw man, I missed you today girl." he says, staring down into her eyes; his arms wrapped firmly around her waist.

Angela returns his squeeze, melting into his arms. He gives the best hugs. They can always take her mind off of her troubles.

"Alright baby, I'm here! I got the movies , I got the popcorn, let's do this!" He laughs, as he pulls her towards the living room for movie night.

"What's all this?" He stops as he passes the table covered in past due bills.

"It's nothing!" Angela says embarrassed that she forgot to put them away. She quickly organizes the pile into a neat stack and shoves it towards the far end of the table.

The pair head into the living room where they pop in the first movie and snuggle up on the couch.

"I'm not staying up too late tonight," Angela warns. "I have to work tomorrow."

An hour later the movie roars on as Will notices Angela has fallen asleep on the couch. He gently kisses her forehead as he hops up and heads to the kitchen to refill his soda.

As he walks past the kitchen table he notices the stack of bills that Angela had attempted to hide from him. He grabs them and goes through each one.

Past due, past due, cut off notice, 30 day notice.

He peeks back into the living room to make sure his fiancé is still sleeping before taking a seat at the table. Will picks up Angela's light bill and pulls out his cell phone. He quickly dials the 800 number on the bill and pulls his credit card out of his wallet.

A few days later Angela finds herself standing in line at Memphis Light Gas and Water. She received a cutoff notice from them days ago and tomorrow her lights are due to be shut off. Lately she's been trying to play catch up on her bills since she had gotten behind while David was living with her.

She recently found out that not only was he sponging off of her but he also maxed out all of her credit cards.
The harassment of the bill collectors was beginning to be more than she could bear.

"Next!" The woman behind the counter calls to Angela.

Angela nervously steps forward rapidly trying to piece together what she's going to say to get an extension on her bill.

"Yes, um, my bill is past due and I - " Angela starts.

"Account number," the woman interrupts, staring blankly at Angela as if her time is somehow being wasted.

Angela, annoyed by the woman's attitude, hands her the bill.

The clerk grabs the bill and types the account number in the computer.

"Ok, what do you need?" She asks with a blank expression.

"I was wondering if I can have a little more time to pay my bill." Angela asks as nicely as she can attempting to hide how annoyed she is with the clerks attitude.

"Uh, ma'am, this account is paid in full." The clerk says while staring at the screen.

"What? No, there must be a mistake, I just got this cut off notice earlier this week. " Angela says pointing at the bill.

"Well, we just received a payment two days ago. You have a zero balance." The clerk prints out a statement showing Angela's account number with a the balance showing 0.00. She hands it to Angela whose feet are frozen to the floor as she stares at the statement in disbelief.

"Next!" The clerk calls, as she ushers Angela out of the way.

Joy is standing in line at the grocery store with Jonathan. These pregnancy cravings have them on a constant hunt for snacks and junk food.

"That'll be $10.93," the cashier says to Jonathan as he pulls out his debit card.

He swipes card and punches in his pin.
The cashier gets an embarrassed look on her face as she leans in to Jonathan.
"I'm sorry sir, your card was declined."

Jonathan feels all of the blood rush to his face. He looks over at Joy who is rolling her eyes. He fishes around in his pocket for some cash as he feels a line of people staring at him.

"Um, can I put some of these back?" he asks, as he attempts to pull some of the items from the bags.

"Ugh! This is pathetic ..." Joy mumbles as she throws a twenty dollar bill on the counter and storms out of the store.

A few moments later, Jonathan emerges from the store bags in hand. He finds Joy leaning against his car with her arms folded. He unlocks the doors and the two enter the vehicle.

"Can I have my change?" She asks staring at the dashboard.

Jon digs the money out of his pocket and hands it to her.

"Look, I'm sorry if I embarrassed you," he says.

"How in the hell am I supposed to raise a child with a man who can't buy 10.00 worth of snacks?" She asks as she looks at him in disgust.

"Damn, get off my back! I just paid my rent and my car insurance, I didn't know my account was down that low! I get paid Friday." Jon yells, his fists clenching the steering wheel as he pulls out of the parking lot.

"So is this how my life is gonna be when we get married? Living from paycheck to paycheck? I can't do this!" Joy screams at him with tears in her eyes.

"I know you can't! That's cause you're weak! Ya ass ain't never had to work for nothin. You don't understand how people whose parents don't have a million dollars in the bank can function, huh?"

Stunned, Joy looks at Jonathan. He had never spoken to her this way.

"Weak? No, I think I'm strong. As a matter a fact I'm strong enough to dump your broke, low class ass before you can marry me and ruin my credit!" Joy strikes back in a vicious tone.

Jonathan slowly comes to a stop outside of Joys house.

Joy climbs out of the car as Jon speeds off before she can slam the door.

Carla finds herself once again parked outside of Albert's office.

She watches as he leaves for lunch with one his business associates.

She moves her car, which has been hidden in the back of the lot out of view, and drives right up to the front door and hops out.

As she heads inside she is greeted by Heather.

"Why Carla, so nice to see you again! What can I do for you?" Heather smiles and bats her eyes.

Carla walks directly up to Heathers desk.

"You can stop sleeping with my husband." Carla looks Heather straight in the eye.

"My, my, aren't we bold today?" Heather says, her smile has never been wider.

"I've decided to give my marriage another chance and if we're going to make a serious effort at this we can't have any distractions." Carla says with one hand on her hip as she uses the other to slide off her Prada shades.

"Oh you've decided?" Heather asks arrogantly. "And, what does Albert think about this?" She furrows her brow.

"I didn't come here for an argument, I came to let you know that whatever it is that you two had is over." Carla remains firm even though she's unsure of how Albert feels at the moment.

Heather stands up, straightens her red pencil skirt, and walks around the front of her desk to stand face to face with Carla.

"Look bitch, I don't know if you came down here to intimidate me or try to scare me off but hear this, I don't scare easily. And besides, if you we're doing everything you need to be doing as a wife, you wouldn't feel the need to come down here and make threats."

Carla remains calm and doesn't flinch a muscle as Heather gets in her face.

"You are truly a pitiful and pathetic person. Any woman who valued herself would never sleep with another woman's husband. You can try to justify it by saying his wife isn't handling her business at home or you may even say it's just about the sex.

But the truth is you are just a pitiful, scared, little girl who is too afraid to venture out there in the real world and find your own man. You feel that at the end of the day its safer to attach yourself to someone who you know deep in your heart will never be yours."

Heather's confidence begins to crack as she fidgets with the edge of the desk. She's finding it harder to look Carla in the eye.

"Look, when I first started here, I didn't know he was married. He came on to me." Heather blurts out trying not to lose her edge.

"That doesn't matter, I came here to tell you that whatever you had with him is over. We are going to make our marriage work. " Carla states again firmly.

"Look, I don't..." Heather starts with a little too much attitude.

"I said what I had to say, it's over!" Carla yells at her. She slides her shades back on her face and turns to walk out of the room. Heather, overcome with emotion, grabs the picture frame on her desk and hurls it across the room at Carla. It smashes against the wall next to her.

Carla spins around and looks over her shades at Heather. "You better get someone to clean that up," she says, as she winks at Heather, chuckles to herself, and exits the office.

CHAPTER 3

Angela has spent the morning on the phone with her bill collectors. All of her balances have been wiped out. She sits in her living room with tears of joy streaming down her face.

At that moment Jonathan knocks on the front door and uses his key to quickly open it. He walks in to find his mom in tears. He rushes to her side.

"Ma, what happened?" He asks

"I don't know." Angela replies through her tears. She hands him a stack of bills. "They're paid . . . all of 'em."

"That's a good thing Ma, why you crying?" Jonathan asks confused.

"Because, I don't know how it happened, it's like yesterday my lights are about to be cut off and my car is getting repossessed, and today everyone I call says I don't owe anything." Angela smiles through her tears.

The door bell rings.

"Well, I guess God does answer prayers. I'll get that Ma, I think you need a minute, anyway." He chuckles, as he hops up to answer the door.

"What's up man," Will says as he enters the house shaking hands with Jonathan.

Jonathan has come to have a deep respect for Will. He has never seen his mom so happy. In fact he's never even liked any of her boyfriends, this one seems to really care about her.

"What's up Will, Moms is in the living room. Watch out, she's a little emotional right now though." Jon laughs, as he ushers Will in the other room.

"Emotional?" Will shares a laugh with Jon as he walks into the living room.

"Oh, hey, baby!" Angela tries to quickly wipe the tears from her face.

"I forgot we had a lunch date, just let me freshen up, I'll be ready in a minute." She says as she hops up, kisses him on the cheek, and tries to head to the bathroom to wash her face.

Will grabs her before she can walk away.

"You ok, baby?" He asks pulling her close to him.

"I'm fine, I just found out all of my bills were paid off! I don't know how it happened but I'm afraid to tell them there must be a mistake." Angela laughs.

"Oh yea, I took care of that for you babe." Will smiles kindly at her.

"You took care of what?" Angela looks confused.

"Your bills. I saw them on the table and I could tell how stressed out you were so...." Will explains, but Angela cuts him off.

"Excuse me! So you snooped through my mail? Are you crazy? Or, just stupid!" Angela's rage is fueled by her embarrassment. She hadn't planned on sharing with Will how terrible her finances were, at least not yet.

Jonathan hides himself in the kitchen listening to the argument.

"Hey! Stop talking before you say something you'll regret!" Will yells sternly as he grabs her upper arms tightly to calm her.

"I didn't mean to embarrass you or piss you off. Look we're engaged now, your stress is my stress! I'm not the type of man that sits back and watches my woman struggle, certainly not my wife! Or should I say, soon to be wife." He smiles at her as he loosens his grip on her arms.

"Baby, I love you. I was just trying to help."

Angela feels her heart melt. She had never had a man do anything close to that for her before. She had spent so many years taking care of sorry men that she couldn't even recognize when one was trying to take care of her. She smiles back at him as a grateful tear streams down her cheek.

"I love you too," she says, as she grabs on to him and squeezes as tight as she can.

Jon smiles to himself as he peeks around the corner. He quietly sneaks out of the house before he's noticed.

Jonathan drags himself up the steps to his apartment. It's been another long day; 8:00 am class and he spent the rest of his day flipping burgers.

He turns the key and opens the front door.

The apartment is dark except for the soft glow of the light coming from the television. Jon suddenly notices he's not alone in the room.

He hears moaning and giggling coming from the sofa to his right. In the shadow he sees Chris kissing and caressing a young woman in the darkness.

"My bad bro," Jonathan says as he heads for his bedroom. Chris ignores him and keeps his attention locked on the young lady who lets out another giggle that stops Jon in his tracks.

He squints through the darkness and focuses on her face.

"Joy?" Jon says in shock.

Joy smiles at him as she reaches over and turns on the lamp.

"Hey," she says as she leans in and kisses Chris on the cheek.

Chris pulls his brush from his pocket and begins brushing his hair with a cocky grin.

"What's up bro?" Chris smiles at him.

Jonathan stands before them unable to speak. His nostrils flaring and fists clenched.

Suddenly a wave of calm rushes over him.
"So what's the plan, are we supposed to fight now?" He asks Joy calmly.

"Am I supposed to cry, beg you to come back to me?"

Joy tries to mask her surprise. She thought for sure this would send him over the edge.

"I don't care what you do." She lies.

Jon looks at Chris and smiles.

"The lease is in my name nigga, you can get ya' ass out of my house . . . and take this ho' with you." He turns and heads to his bedroom and slams the door.

Carla and Albert are leaving their first therapy session; they head down the sidewalk towards their separate vehicles.

"You have to talk more, Albert. I told you I would sign the papers if you gave it an effort!" You can't just sit there looking at your watch." Carla stomps to her car angrily.

"I was sitting there thinking about how ridiculous this whole thing is. You tried to kill me a few months ago and now we're just supposed to go to couples therapy and that makes it all better, you're delusional! I don't know if I believe this marriage is worth saving!" Albert let's out an annoyed sigh.

"Of course you don't think our marriage can be saved! That's because you're still sleeping with that tramp! She is clouding up your mind, Albert! You'll never know what you want as long as she is in the picture! You need to get rid of her and I mean it!" Carla warns.

"Oh, so now you wanna play wife?" Albert says angrily. "Now that you're threatened that another woman might actually knock you off your perch, *NOW* you wanna act like a wife. Where has my wife been for the last 19 years, huh?" Albert fires back at her.

Carla stands next to her car and slides on her favorite Prada shades.

"Get that whore out of our lives or . . ." Carla starts.

"Or what?" Albert asks cutting her off mid sentence.

"You heard me," Carla responds, her brown eyes staring daggers at him.

"No, I'll tell you what. How about I get you out of my life, How about I just write you a check for the money you wanted and we can just end this right now." Albert screams in her face.

"End this? You said you were willing to work on us. That's why we came here." Carla says, her ego clearly bruised.

Albert scribbles out a check and hands it to her.
"You're not worth the trouble," he marches off to his car without looking back.

Carla rips up the check and tosses the pieces into the wind. She climbs in her white BMW and speeds off. Her tires screeching and echoing through the parking lot.

David pulls into the driveway of Angela's house in his work truck. He's been making deliveries for FedEx and unbelievably, he's held a steady job for the past four months.

It's been two months since Angela told him she was engaged. The thought of her getting married has been slowly torturing him, made worse only by the fact that she no longer takes his calls or texts.

He knows that this time has to be different from the many other times that she cut him off. Usually he can find a way to weasel his way back into her good graces. Not this time. This time feels final and much to his own surprise, he's not willing to accept that.

He hops out of the car and walks right up to the front door. He pauses for a moment before ringing the bell as if rethinking his choice to show up unannounced.

He hears the ding dong of the doorbell echo throughout the house.

Angela peeks through the window. She opens the door without taking off the chain.

"David! What are you doing here, are you crazy? I tell you to stop calling me so you show up at my house unannounced? What if my man was here?" Angela yells, infuriated.

"Slow down, Angie. Damn! I just wanted to see you. Is that so wrong?" David gives her a half smile.

"Yes, yes it is SO wrong. I'm engaged, David. I can't be playing these games with you." She gives him an annoyed stare.

"Look, ughh!" He stumbles to find the right words.

"I miss you, I miss my friend. I just want to talk to you. Can we talk?" He nudges on the door, his eyes asking if he can come inside.

Angela laughs to herself. As she thinks back over her past with David.

"There it is," she smiles. "That is how you get me every time. I allow you to put me in this "friend" box. Pretty soon, I'm your shoulder to cry on. I'm your counselor, Hell, I'm even the one you call when something funny happens during the day. Then I end up exactly where I don't wanna be . . . in love with you." Her eyes fight back tears.

"And you are just not capable of loving me back, at least not the way I need to be loved."

"Angie, it's not like that this time. I've had a lot of time to think and I realize how much I put you through. I'm sorry . . . for everything." His eyes drop to the ground.

Angela takes the chain off of the door, steps half way out of the house, she tightens her robe around her waist and folds her arms across her chest.

"Ok, apology accepted. Anything else?" She says, staring blankly at him.

"Look, Angie, I ain't trying to cause problems between you and your man. I just miss you." He says with sincerity as he reaches out and puts one arm around her waist.

Angela feels her heart flutter as he touches her. His touch is so comfortable, so familiar.

She takes a step back and slowly takes his hand off her waist.

"I miss you too. But I can't do this again."

She steps back inside of the house and closes the door.

CHAPTER 4

Chris turns the key to his new apartment. He pushes the door open and ushers Joy inside.

Chris' parents have rented him an apartment in downtown Memphis with a view of the Mississippi river.

Joy steps inside, her eyes smiling as she takes a look around the luxury apartment.

"This is amazing," Joy says, as she looks around the fully furnished, freshly painted, apartment home.

"See this is how my man should be living. I was getting sick and tired of Jon inviting me to that hell hole you two were living in."

"Don't talk to me about Jon," Chris says grabbing her tightly. "I don't wanna think about Jon and I don't want you thinking about Jon. You're my woman now." He says as he relaxes his grip on her arm.

Joy steps back, pulling her arm from his grasp.

"Ok, fine." She says uneasily.

He wraps his arms around her waist and pulls her close to him.

"I'm sorry baby. I guess I just spent too much time watching you kissing and touching him. I just don't want you thinking about him anymore." He says kissing her cheek.

"Besides, I wanted to ask you something," he smiles romantically.

"What do think about moving in with me?"

"Oh my God!" Joy squeals. "Yes, let's do it!" She grabs his face kissing him passionately.

Carla walks down the isle of her grocery store. She pushes a wobbly shopping cart through the store while throwing random items in the basket.

"Where is he?" she whispers to herself, as she pretends to shop.

His name was Marcus Jackson but in the streets he's known only as "Black." A local hood Carla remembered from her days as an attorney. She got him out of hot water a few years back.

She spots him heading her way, seeming to have appeared almost from thin air. As he walks past her they greet as if old friends, smile and say their hellos, then share a friendly embrace. Carla slides a white envelope in the pocket of his coat. She whispers in his ear before he moves away.

"I only want her scared, nothing more."

He winks at Carla before heading on his way.

Carla ditches the basket and heads for the exit.

Two days later Carla walks calmly down the hall of St Francis Hospital.

An hour earlier she'd received a message from Black, one word: "St Francis."

"Hi, I'm looking for a friend of mine." Carla says, as she somberly approaches the front desk.

"Heather Peters. I got a call that she was attacked," Carla explains, as the tears spill down her cheeks.

"Yes. She's in 1016," the receptionist says after typing the name in her data base.

"It's down the hall on the right."

Carla's heels click clack down the cold sterile hall. She approaches room 1016 and peeks through the window.

"She a friend of yours?" A voice from behind startles her. She turns to see a man in a white lab coat standing there.

"Um, yea." Carla responds awkwardly.

"You just missed the family. I told them to go home and get some rest. They've been here all night." He says, his kind eyes smiling sympathetically.

"It's terrible that a woman can't even feel safe in her own home these days."

"What happened to her?" Carla asks innocently.

"Police say someone broke in while she was sleeping. The guy raped her and beat her up pretty bad." The doctor explains.

"Raped her?" Carla feels a knot in her stomach.

"Yea, she's got a broken nose, and a dislocated jaw. Her hip bone is broken in two places. The doctor says looking down at his chart.

"I was about to check on her, but I'll give you a minute. Go on in, I'll be back in a moment."

As the doctor glides down the hall, Carla takes a deep breath, pushes the door open and walks inside.

Her heart sinks as she sees Heather lying there all bandaged up. She only told Black to scare her, she never thought that he would take it this far.

"Who's there?" Heather eeks the words out through clinched teeth, her jaw having been wired shut.

Carla, although startled, is not about to lose face. She shakes off her emotions and walks right up to the side of the bed.

Heather looks confused as she squints at Carla through a blackened eye.

"I heard you had a little accident, I just came to see how you're doing." She says smiling down at her.

"Why....are... you... here?" Heather mumbles through the wire.

"I guess this means my husband and I won't be seeing you for a while. That's a shame." Carla smirks vindictively.

"Get...out!" Heather grunts as hard as she can, tears roll down the side of her face into her hair.

Just then a nurse walks in carrying a pitcher of ice water.

Carla gently touches Heather's arm.

"You stay strong, I'll see you soon." She winks as she turns and heads for the door.

Angela and Will are having dinner by candlelight as Luther Vandross plays on the radio.

Will takes her hand, kisses it gently, and nuzzles it against his face. Its times like this that make celibacy extremely difficult. The deeper they connect spiritually and emotionally the harder it is to resist each other physically.

Will grabs her hand and pulls her out of her chair over to his side of the table. Looking in her eyes he pulls her down on his lap. Angela slowly kisses her man as Will's massive hands caress her back.

She's never felt so safe, so comfortable with a man in her life.

Ding dong!

The doorbell sounds off, stopping them just as things are about to go too far.

Angela laughs and lays her head on his shoulder as Will rolls his eyes and smiles to himself.

"I'll get that" she smiles at him and kisses his cheek before heading off to the door.

As Angela walks to the door, she hears tires screeching away. She looks through the window and sees no one there. She's about to chalk it up to neighborhood kids until she looks down and notices a bouquet of red roses sitting in a glass vase on her porch.

"Who is it baby?" Will calls from the dining room.

Angela walks around the corner carrying the flowers.

"No one was there, but I found these on the porch." She says, as she sits the vase on the table.

Will notices a card sticking out of the flowers. He pulls it out and opens it.

It reads:

"I'm not giving up on us."

- David

Will snatches the vase off of the table and rushes outside. He runs down the driveway stopping next to the mailbox. His nostrils flaring like an angry bull as his eyes search up and down the street for David.

Angela rushes out to his side.

"Will! Baby come back in the house, he's gone." She cries, pulling him back toward the house.

Will snatches away from her and throws the vase in the street. Angela watches as it smashes into what seems like a billion pieces.

"You better tell him to stay his ass away from you!" Will yells into the night air, his eyes doing one last search of the street before he charges back up the driveway and into the house.

Angela stands in the driveway, her face wet with tears. She hates seeing Will this angry.

A small part of her feels guilty although she knows that she did everything she could to make it clear to David that she had moved on. Angela can't help but wonder why David is still coming after her. Then a thought comes to her that she instantly tries to suppress.

"Maybe he has changed, maybe seeing me happy with another man finally gave him the realization that I am a good woman. Maybe if we try again we can make it work." Her mind wanders.

Just as she gets lost in a sea of "maybes" a car rushes past her snapping her back to reality.

Angela stares at the smashed vase and all of the beautiful long stemmed roses now laying in the street. She finds herself wanting to touch at least one of them.

She glances back at the house before walking out into the middle of the street where they lay. She bends over and grabs a single rose out of the pile. Angela holds the rose up to her nose as she gazes into the darkness. The smell of it brings a smile to her face.

She plucks a few of the petals off of the stem and quickly shoves them in her pocket before tossing the stem back into the pile.

Angela saunters slowly up the driveway. As she gets to the front door she turns again to the darkness of the night and smiles as the wind blows through her hair. She steps inside and closes the door.

Joy is leaning against the sink washing dishes in the apartment that she now shares with Chris.

Chris walks up behind her and gently sweeps her hair over to one side and softly kisses her neck as he wraps his arms around her.

"Babe, I could've done the dishes. I don't need my girl slaving away in the kitchen while she's carrying my child." He whispers as he kisses her neck.

Joy smiles as she gives him a quick peck on the cheek.

"Uh huh, you would say this when I'm almost done." She laughs.

Her phone buzzes from its perch on top of the microwave. Chris grabs it quickly before Joy has a chance to reach for it.

Jonathan has sent a text asking if he can come with her to her doctor's appointment in the morning. He knows this is when she'll find out the sex of the baby.

Chris reads the text and immediately begins to see red. He holds the screen up to Joy's face.

"What the hell is this?" He yells.

Joy dries her hands on her pants and grabs the phone.

"He wants to come to the appointment, what the hell is your problem?" She rolls her eyes as she slams the phone on the counter.

"I thought I told you not to talk to him anymore! I thought I told you you're my woman now! My woman ain't gon' be talking to another man, period!" He pins her against the counter screaming in her face.

Joy, is beginning to get nervous about Chris's controlling behavior but no one talks to her like that and gets away with it.
"And who the hell do you think you are? You don't talk to me like that!" She screams even louder than he had.

"I will do whatever the hell........"

Chris balls his fist and punches Joy in the face before she can finish her sentence. The punch knocks her to the floor. She sits up and looks at him in shock. Her eyes searching his for any hint of the charming charismatic guy she was falling in love with.

There's no sign of him, all she sees is an angry stranger staring back at her. She tries to crawl away but he grabs her by the hair and slams her against the counter.

"You think I'm stupid, bitch!" He slaps her across the face.

"You still talking to him, ain't you? You think I'm stupid, don't you!" Chris slaps and kicks Joy around the kitchen while she screams and begs him to stop.

He grabs her hair and slams her to the floor. He snatches her cell phone from the counter and smashes it against the wall.

Chris walks over to sink and grabs a blue plastic cup. He turns on the faucet and fills the cup about halfway. Chris's normally fair skinned hand is now purple and swollen. He guzzles down the water and throws the cup in the sink.

He walks past Joy who is sobbing uncontrollably while curled up in a ball on the floor.

He leans over and spits on her, it lands on her shoulder and dribbles down her back.

"Tell that nigga to quit textin' you," he grumbles, as he walks out of the room.

Stay tuned for the next part of the Joy series!

Miss any part of the Joy series? Catch up today!

www.KimJKirby.com

About the Author

Kimberly Kirby is an American author who resides in Memphis, TN. She writes poetry, children's books, songs, and scripts for the silver screen. Kimberly is also the author of **What to Do Until He Finds You** and the ***Joy series.***

Behind the Scenes

of Kimberly Kirby's "Joy Series"

I am so proud of the success that I have had from my book series, "Joy." It's is so gratifying to put your heart into something you love and have people actually "get" it and love it.

I wanted to take time to share with you why I wrote the "Joy" Series and give you a little more background on the story.

First off, very few people know this about me but I have always wanted to write a television show that speaks to and connects African American women. A show that was both entertaining and relevant to what we go through every day.

Since I don't currently have the connections or the resources to produce a major television show, I decided to write it. I don't actually consider myself a "novelist". When you read The "Joy" Series, you'll find that the books are a combination of a TV script and a traditional book.

Second, you'll find that there is a little bit of me in each one of the female lead characters. No, I'm not saying that the characters' actions and situations are actually things that I've done or been through (for the most part). However, those that know me well will recognize that SOME of the ways the characters respond to certain situations would mirror the way I would respond.

While writing the books, I wanted to make the storyline seem as real as possible so from time to time I would drop myself in that scenario and let my natural reaction flow through the pages.

Fun Fact: While writing the scene where Angela sees David in the grocery store, I was literally in tears. This is one of my favorite scenes in the entire series. When she was yelling "Say something, Say something" In her mind but didn't have the courage or the strength to say it out loud; That was definitely a Kim moment.

I was once told, What comes from the heart reaches the heart. That couldn't be more true in this case. This series was definitely written from my heart and every time someone tells me that it has touched them or spoken to them in some way my heart smiles.

Thank you for reading The "Joy" Series, the best **show** you've ever **read**! – Kimberly Kirby

You Were Supposed to Be Different

(Poetry inspired by The Joy Series)

Screaming in my pillow with tears running down my face

You were supposed to be different.

Everything and everyone around you whispered to my spirit that

you were different.

Your walk was that of a king,

your speech had that perfect combination of intelligence and

slang.

Finally a man who can carry on a decent conversation about life

and love and faith.

Yet I was deceived, and once again I ended up in the same place.

Screaming in my pillow with tears running down my face.

You were supposed to be different, everything and everyone

around you whispered to my spirit that you were different.

Tired of the dating scene, you said you were ready to settle down.

Said that I was the type of woman that a king could give his crown to. So I waited, and watched as you abused my heart over and over again until my heart could no longer take it, or maybe just refused to fake it. So no longer will my time be wasted. Because our pitiful excuse of a relationship forced me to face it.

I'm Screaming in my pillow with tears running down my face because

I was supposed to be different.

What is it in me that would give you that much power over my happiness?

I was supposed to be different.

Why would I allow you to treat me as anything less than the Proverbs 31 woman that I am, whose value is far above rubies.

I was supposed to be different.

Now I realize that the spirit that was inside of you couldn't handle the spirit that was inside of me.

I was supposed to be different.

I was chosen, called and set apart for my husband, and brotha you ain't even good enough to be my cousin.

I AM different

So no sir, I have no more time to waste and never again will I end up in that place,

Screaming in my pillow with tears running down my face saying .

.. you were supposed to be different.

I Love You (Joys' Story)

(Poetry inspired by The Joy Series)

You show up at my door with flowers, you shake hands with my dad, kiss my mom on the cheek, and we leave.

Out on the town, you take me to my favorite restaurant. At the end of the meal I reach for my wallet and you say nah baby, I got this. You take me home, we make sweet passionate love until we fall asleep. I wake up smiling. I look over to your side of the bed . . . and you're gone.

And see that's where I get confused, and then I start to feel used.

You want me when you want me, you need it, when you need it. And then you tell me to beat it.

And I admit that's when I get a little heated.

Cause all you see is this cute little smile on my face and I know I haven't shown you that other side me yet, but trust me, you don't want these problems.

I can make things real difficult for you. But I don't want to cause I love you.

I have that crazy, passionate, deep, almost psychopathic love for you.

See I love you with that I don't care type love

I love you with that let'em stare type love

I love you with that (whew!) I'll follow you anywhere type love.

All you have to do is accept the fact that this is going to happen.

You and I will be together.

See I'm like an anaconda, the more you struggle the harder I squeeze.

But I promise you the love I have will bring you to your knees.

I am the type of woman that will treat you like a king.

All you have to do is let me.

www.ingramcontent.com/pod-product-compliance
Lightning Source LLC
Chambersburg PA
CBHW070529130626
46555CB00003B/1339